THANK YOU
Fernando Escoto, deputy director of CONAMP
(the government commission to protect the Valley of the Cirios),
for your enormous help throughout and Maria Luisa Uribe Meza
for your inspiration.

I also wish to thank
Vanessa Ahlberg, Haydn Washington,
Lily Callanan, Jim Hood, Liz Seymour,
and the many other friends who helped.

Francisco Javier Delgadillo Peralta acted the part of the boy in the story.
Marcial Antelmo Gomez Sanchez acted the part of his grandfather.

Copyright © 2023 by Jeannie Baker
Epigraph copyright © 2004 from *The Best of Chief Dan George* by Hancock House
Publishers Ltd. ISBN 978-088839-544-3. Used with permission. www.hancockhouse.com.

All rights reserved. No part of this book may be reproduced, transmitted, or stored
in an information retrieval system in any form or by any means, graphic, electronic,
or mechanical, including photocopying, taping, and recording, without prior written
permission from the publisher.

First US edition 2023
First published by Walker Books Ltd. (UK) 2023

Library of Congress Catalog Card Number 2022908672
ISBN 978-1-5362-2577-8

23 24 25 26 27 28 APS 10 9 8 7 6 5 4 3 2 1

Printed in Humen, Dongguan, China

This book was typeset in Kohinoor Bangla.
The illustrations were done as collage and reproduced from color photographs
by Jamie Plaza.

Candlewick Press
99 Dover Street
Somerville, Massachusetts 02144

www.candlewick.com

Desert Jungle

JEANNIE BAKER

What you do not know, you will fear.
What one fears, one destroys.
Chief Dan George

CANDLEWICK PRESS

In a desert valley, surrounded by mountains
of rock and cacti, is a tiny village. My home.

I never wander far from home
because I think coyotes will take me.
I hear them howling in the night
and the village dogs barking.

Then I go and stay with Grandpa.

He wants to show me the place where he grew up.

It is far from any village.

When we arrive, Grandpa suggests
we go exploring . . .
but I only want to play on my tablet.

That evening,
I leave my bag outside
the ranch house.
It has everything in it,
even the cake my mother
made for us.

But when I go to get the cake . . .
my bag is gone!

I am miserable
without my tablet.
So in the morning,
I go looking for my bag,
not thinking about
where I am going
until I realize . . .

I don't know where I am.

I sense unseen eyes
watching me.
I hear scrunching,
scratching, snapping.
I panic and run.

Thorns catch my clothes
and I stumble,
sprawling in the dust.

I pick myself up and try to stay calm.
After a while, I realize I can see the shape
of the mountain behind the ranch house.
It shows me the way back to Grandpa.

"My bag is gone," I sob. "And this place scares me.
It's a desert jungle!"
Grandpa is impressed that I worked out how
to find my way back.

"Why, chico?" he says.
"Why be afraid?"

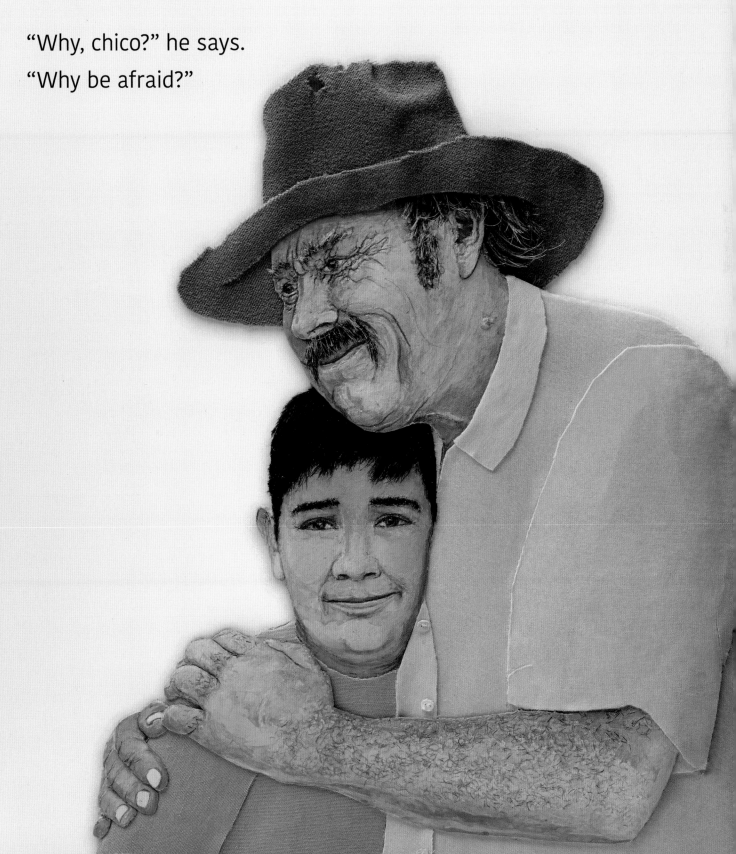

Later, Grandpa takes me exploring.

We walk a long way from the ranch house through the cacti and the scrub.

Grandpa shows me amazing plants . . .
ocotillo, cholla, cirio,
pincushion, fishhook . . .

Suddenly, Grandpa stops and points.

"We won't go closer,"
he whispers.
"Isn't it beautiful!"

On our way back to the ranch house, Grandpa tells me,
"This valley is full of secrets, chico.
Open your heart, listen,
and see what wonders show themselves."

When Grandpa is busy
fixing things on the ranch,
I begin to explore on my own.

While I quietly sit,
watching ants carry leaves,
I hear buzzing,
and for a moment
a hummingbird hovers near my shoulder!

The rocks fascinate me.
When I turn them over, sometimes
I find another world
living underneath.

I start a collection of treasures.
And I start to wander farther away.

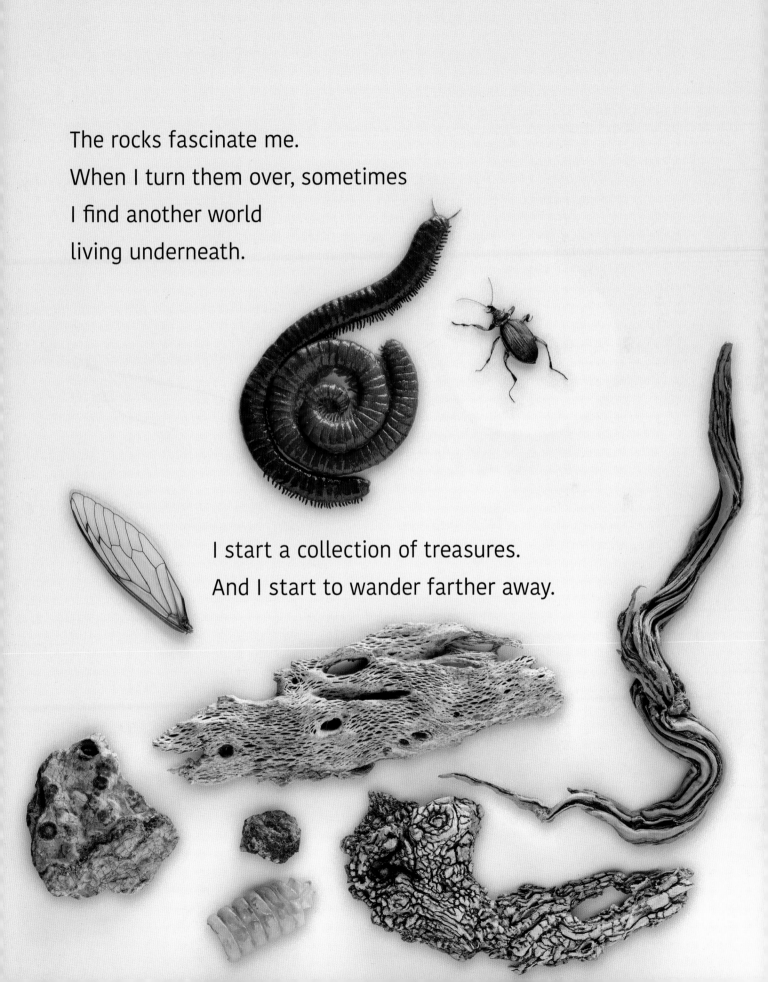

One afternoon, I am walking in the mountains
when the sky suddenly grows dark.
A great wind comes from nowhere,
hurling leaves and branches in the air.

I run into a cave for shelter.

When my eyes adjust
to the darkness,
deep in the shadows
I make out a coyote.
My heart thumps.
Our eyes lock.

There is a thundering
CRASH as a tree falls.

I look back . . .
The coyote is gone.
My heart is still pounding.
Did I imagine it?

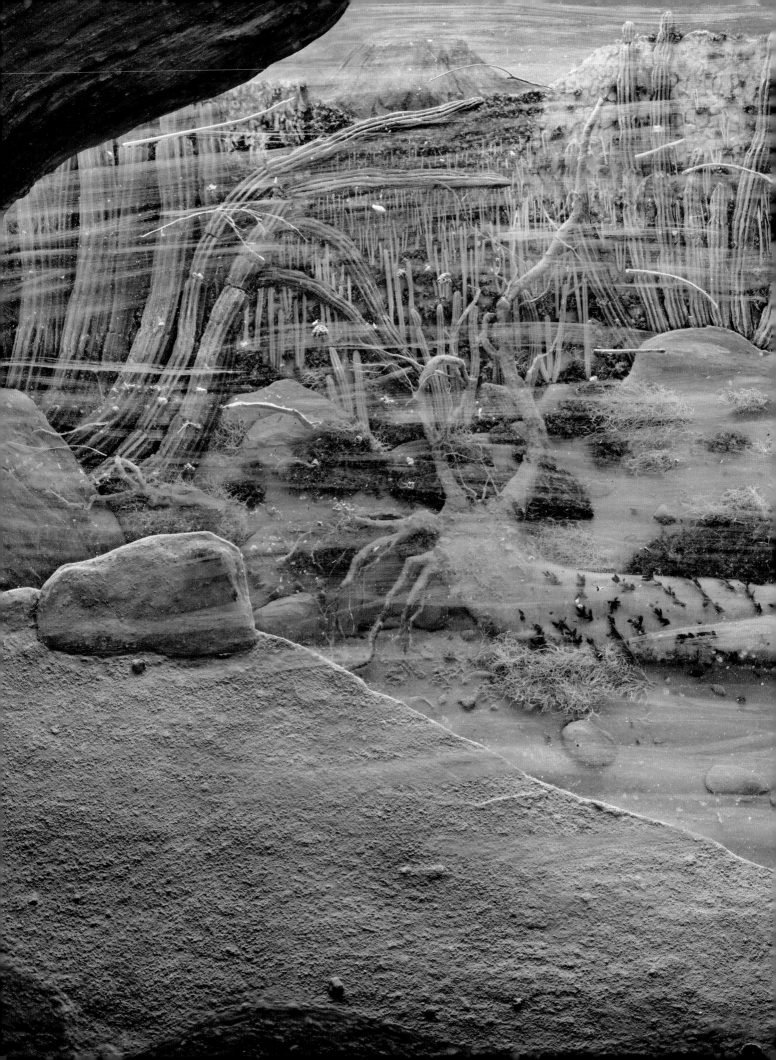

When the wind is quieter, I make my way
back to the ranch house and meet Grandpa.
He's been frantic, looking for me.
I'm glad to see him and tell him about the coyote.

The next day, I take Grandpa to my cave.

"Look, Grandpa, a coyote was here.
See the tracks!"

"Coyote is still here," Grandpa murmurs,
pointing at the wall.

I return to my village
feeling love for my desert home.
I try to give its creatures space . . .
My fear is gone.

At times, I hide in the shadows,
watching, waiting, listening . . .
and sometimes . . .
I am gifted
to see a wonder of the wild.

The Setting

My story takes place in the Sonoran Desert, more specifically in the Valle de los Cirios (Valley of the Cirios), which covers a third of Baja California. It is the largest natural protected area of land in Mexico (but is not as strongly protected as a national park). It is under consideration to be named a UNESCO World Heritage site. This enchanting subtropical desert is named after the cirio—an extraordinary tree that thrives here and gives the valley much of its character. The forms cirios take are often wild and strange: some are thick, some thin; some soar and branch crazily, some droop and curl fantastically; no two are alike. They are also called boojums.

In parts of the valley, towering stands of cardon cacti (some of the largest cacti on Earth) and elephant trees mix with cirios and other unique desert plants to create a "forest"—almost a desert jungle. Amid the desert vegetation live many amazing animals, including mountain lions, bighorn sheep, peninsular pronghorn deer, frogs, chameleons, rattlesnakes, tarantulas, eagles, hawks, and owls. Countless plants and animals (some of which are endangered) can only be found here.

Petroglyphs (carvings) and paintings (some prehistoric) can be found on rocks and in rock shelters and caves. It is believed these were created by different groups of hunter-gatherers and fisherfolk at various times over more than seven thousand years. Whoever the anonymous artists were, they show a deep connection to and celebration of this wild, enchanting landscape. The cave painting of the coyote that the boy discovers in the story is from the Montevideo valley. Despite extensive research, it is unknown who painted it.

The Sonoran Desert is the hottest desert in Mexico. Some years there is no rain at all. Its average annual rainfall is less than 5 inches (125 mm). Most of the rainfall occurs in two rainy seasons—winter and summer. The unusual weather patterns are just one of the reasons why this area is home to great biodiversity, with more plant species than any other desert. Although the region is remote, its ecological integrity is continuously threatened by land sales, subdivisions, mining, tourism, and industrial development.

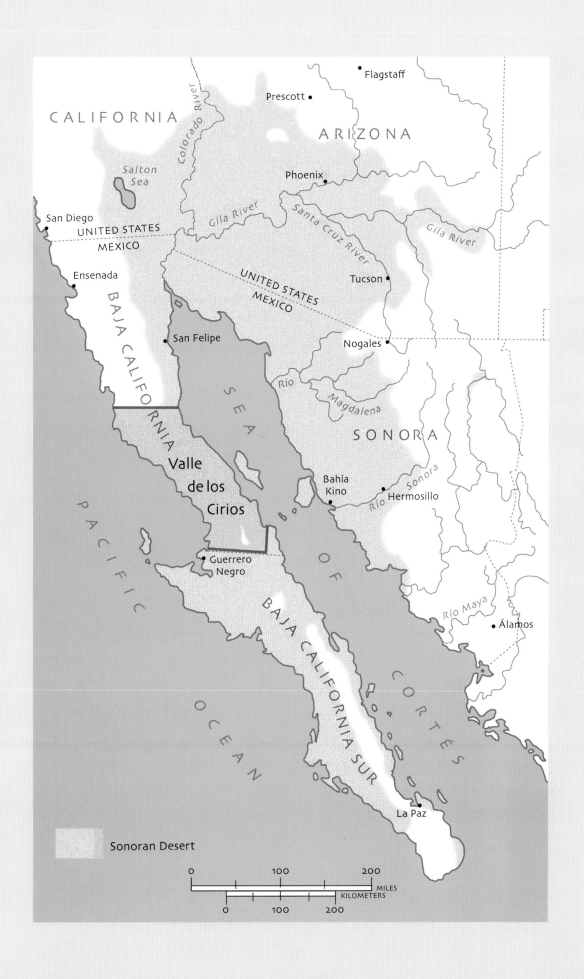

Author's Note

Our preconception of the desert as a barren, desolate, lifeless place needs to be challenged. Recent studies show deserts, not rain forests, are richest in pollinator diversity. The biodiversity of the world's deserts is rapidly disappearing as people who believe deserts to be wastelands unknowingly turn them into one.

In early 2017, drawn by the power of this landscape, I made a six-week research trip to the Sonoran Desert of Baja California and Arizona, where I explored desert landscapes, spoke with locals and scientists, visited museums, and documented this unique environment. I've depicted the desert as it looked then. It was late winter, there had been rain . . . and it was glorious.

In Santa Rosalillita, a fishing village in Baja, I met Maria Luisa Uribe Meza. She had grown up there and then taught at the village school. Maria showed me her master's thesis, which evolved through her personal observation that the children she taught knew little about the local plants and animals, and that the knowledge held by older generations was gradually being lost. The children, she told me, did not have a strong sense of belonging and connection to their home.

Maria's thesis had a profound influence on me. The condition she described, known as "nature-deficit disorder," is a worldwide problem, but I was surprised that it would be a problem here, in a tiny village where the children grow up seemingly surrounded by the power of the natural world. Having always felt a deep sense of wonder toward nature, I went on to develop my story with Maria's support.

A decreasing number of children today grow up incorporating nature into their sense of home. They are often unfamiliar with even the common names of the plants and animals around them. They can feel so distanced from nature that they come to fear it. Nature-deficit disorder isolates children from the living world and breeds indifference toward environmental concerns.

By contrast, children who grow up with an intimate involvement with and a sense of wonder about the life around them learn to respect and care for the natural world and feel more connected to their local environment.

Jeannie Baker